Bravo, Mildred & Ed!

Karen Wagner

Illustrations by
Janet Pedersen

Walker & Company
New York

First published in the United States of America in 2000 by
Walker Publishing Company, Inc.

Published simultaneously in Canada by Fitzhenry and Whiteside, Markham, Ontario L3R 4T8

Library of Congress Cataloging-in-Publication Data
Wagner, Karen.
Bravo, Mildred & Ed! / Karen Wagner ; illustrations by Janet Pedersen.
p. cm.
Summary: Mouse friends Mildred and Ed, pulled apart by different interests, find that
they can successfully do some things together and other things separately.
ISBN 0-8027-8734-7 (hc.)——ISBN 0-8027-8735-5 (rein)
[1. Friendship——Fiction. 2. Mice——Fiction.] I. Title: Bravo, Mildred, and Ed!
II. Pedersen, Janet, ill. III. Title.
PZ7.W12428 Br 2000
[E]——dc21   00-021060

Printed in Hong Kong

2 4 6 8 10 9 7 5 3 1

For Mary Jack — K. W.

For my sisters, Barbara and Lisa — J. P.

~~~~~~~~~~~~~~~~~~~~~~~~~~~~~~~

Mildred and Ed had been friends for as long as anyone could remember. . . .

If you saw Mildred, you could bet that Ed was not far away.

And if you saw Ed, Mildred was bound to be close by.

One Sunday Mildred and Ed were finishing up a kite they had been working on all weekend. Mildred tied the last bow on the tail.

"Ta-da," said Ed. "It's done. Let's go to the park and sail it in the wind."

Mildred looked at the clock. "It's time for me to practice my violin. My teacher, Mr. Arthur, says I need to work on my scales. They are still a little squeaky. A musician must be dedicated, you know."

"You're right," Ed said, trying to sound cheerful. "Practice is most important. We'll fly the kite another time."

Ed walked slowly home.

Sitting on the front-porch steps, Ed sorted buttons. Buttons always made him feel better. Plink. Plink. Plink. They fell into the jar.

"What fabulous buttons," said a voice. "The teal, the turquoise, the purple, the periwinkle! My name is Pauline," the voice announced. "And you, my friend, are an artist."

"I am?" asked Ed.

"We must have a show so everyone can appreciate your collection. It must be Saturday. I will fit you in between the foot photography exhibit and the paper-towel sculptures."

The next morning, Ed and Mildred met at the train station.

"I have wonderful news, the most wonderful news," he told Mildred. "My button collection is going to be in an art show on Saturday."

"It can't be," Mildred said. "Saturday is my recital, and you have to be there."

"Oh no, I was so excited I forgot all about your recital. What will we do?"

Mildred thought for a while. "I have an idea," she said. "We can practice doing things alone and by Saturday we will be very used to it."
"Good idea!" Ed exclaimed. "We'll start with our trip to the city today."

On the train, Ed made up a game of counting everything round in the shape of a button. He stopped after one hundred and forty-three button-shaped objects. He knew Mildred would have been able to help him find more.

In the city, Mildred went to the planetarium. "Oh, how Ed would have loved making wishes on the falling stars," thought Mildred.

At the museum, Ed was certain he saw Mildred's face in some of the paintings.

Ed and Mildred met for lunch. Ed ordered a peanut butter and jelly sandwich without the jelly. Mildred ordered spaghetti and meatballs without the meatballs. "We are practicing doing things alone," Ed told the waiter.

Over lunch Mildred confessed, "I am a little afraid of playing my violin in front of strangers."

Ed handed Mildred a shiny purple button.

"But that is your favorite button," Mildred said. "The first one you ever found."

"It's yours . . . for luck," Ed said.

Mildred smiled and put the button in her pocket.

The next week, Ed and Mildred did all of the things they could think of that could be done alone.

It was a lonely week.

On Friday morning, Mildred practiced her violin. She did not tremble on her tremolo. Her pizzicato was perfect.

"Magnificent, my dear," proclaimed Mr. Arthur.

But Mildred did not feel magnificent.

On Friday afternoon, Ed set up his art show.
He looked at his collection, but the colors just didn't seem bright today.

That night Mildred tossed and turned.
She tried everything to fall asleep.

She read a book.

She drank warm milk.

She even tried counting buttons,
but nothing helped.

Ed was up late working.
Suddenly he heard a
sound coming from
outside his window. It
was Mildred!

"If you cannot come to
the concert," Mildred
said, "I will bring the
concert to you."

"And you will be with
me at the button show," Ed replied. "Look!"

The next night, Mildred peered out from behind the curtain. Her stomach was flip-flopping, her palms were sweating, her knees were knocking.

As she nervously tugged on her dress, she felt a small round lump in her pocket. Ed's lucky button!

Finally the curtain opened. Mr. Arthur cleared his throat and tapped his baton. Mildred played her very best, without any squeaking at all.

At the gallery, Ed watched while everyone admired his button collection. And as they gathered around his favorite portrait, Ed was sure he could hear music that was sweet and wonderful.

The next day, Ed and Mildred went to the park. "We can do anything," Mildred boasted happily.

"Yes we can," added Ed. "But most of all I enjoy the things we do together."

"So do I," said Mildred. She looked at the sky. "It looks like a fine day to fly a kite."

"I think you're right," said Ed. "A fine day to fly a kite with a best friend."